SONIC™ THE HEDGEHOG

FALLOUT PART 4

WRITTEN BY IAN FLYNN ART BY EVAN STANLEY
COLORS BY MATT HERMS LETTERS BY COREY BREEN
EDITED BY JOE HUGHES & DAVID MARIOTTE PUBLISHED BY GREG GOLDSTEIN

ABDO Spotlight IDW

ABDOBOOKS.COM

Reinforced library bound edition published in 2020 by Spotlight, a division of ABDO, PO Box 398166, Minneapolis, Minnesota 55439. Spotlight produces high-quality reinforced library bound editions for schools and libraries.
Published by agreement with IDW.

Printed in the United States of America, North Mankato, Minnesota.
092019
012020

THIS BOOK CONTAINS
RECYCLED MATERIALS

Library of Congress Control Number: 2019942014

Publisher's Cataloging-in-Publication Data

Names: Flynn, Ian, author. | Yardley, Tracy; Amash, Jim; Hernandez, Jennifer; Thomas, Adam Bryce; Stanley, Evan; Breckel, Heather; Herms, Matt; Smith, Bob, illustrators.
Title: Fallout / writer: Ian Flynn; art: Tracy Yardley; Jim Amash; Jennifer Hernandez; Adam Bryce Thomas; Evan Stanley; Heather Breckel; Matt Herms; Bob Smith
Description: Minneapolis, Minnesota: Spotlight, 2020 | Series: Sonic the Hedgehog
Summary: In the aftermath of his latest battle with Dr. Eggman, Sonic and his friends must defend small villages around the world against robot attacks.
Identifiers: ISBN 9781532144332 (pt. 1, lib. bdg.) | ISBN 9781532144349 (pt. 2, lib. bdg.) | ISBN 9781532144356 (pt. 3, lib. bdg.) | ISBN 9781532144363 (pt. 4, lib. bdg.)
Subjects: LCSH: Sonic the Hedgehog--(Fictitious character)--Juvenile fiction. | Hedgehogs--Juvenile fiction. | Video game characters--Juvenile fiction. | Good and evil--Juvenile fiction. | Graphic novels--Juvenile fiction. | Comic books, strips, etc.-- Juvenile fiction
Classification: DDC 741.5--dc23

Spotlight
A Division of ABDO
abdobooks.com

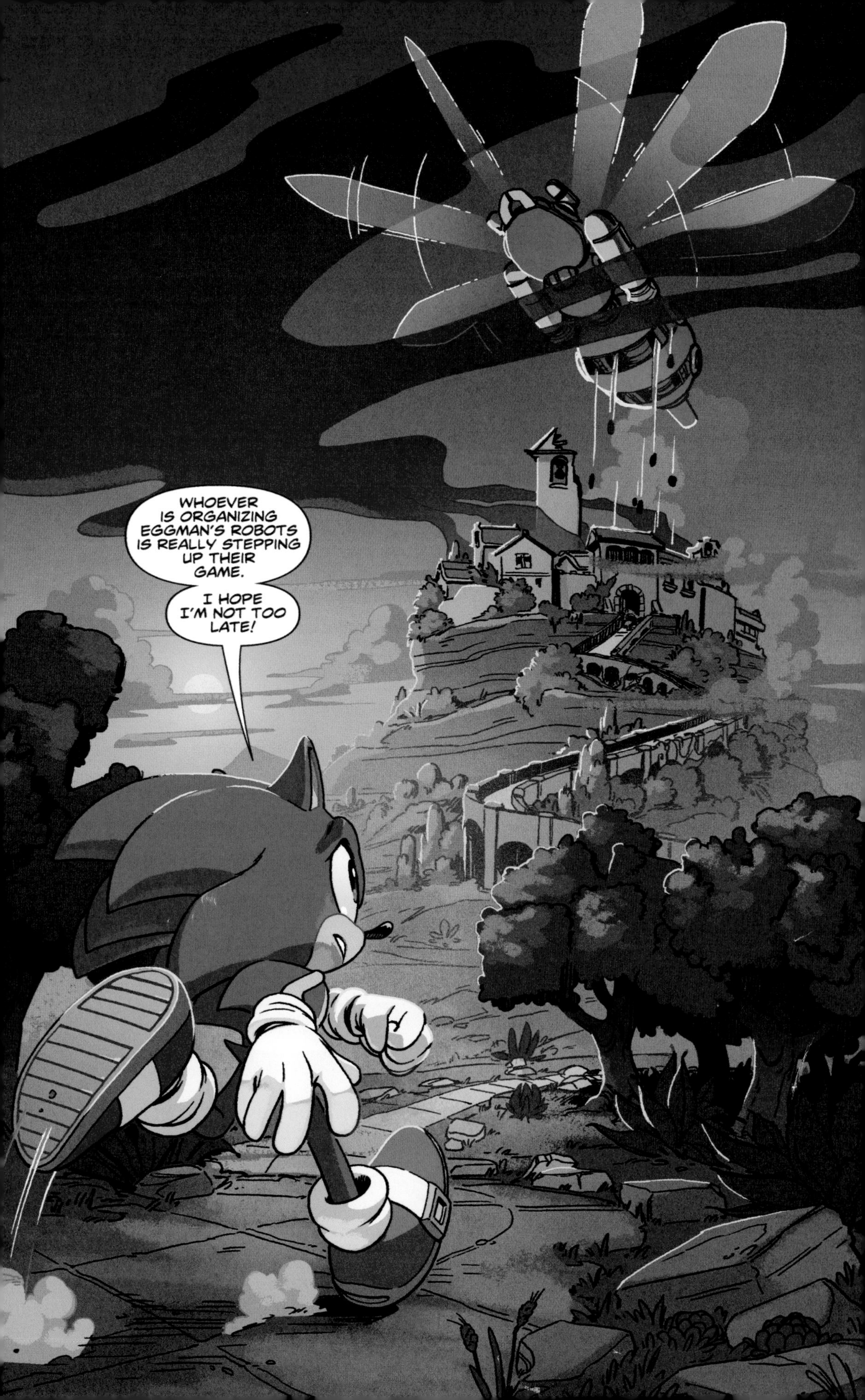
WHOEVER IS ORGANIZING EGGMAN'S ROBOTS IS REALLY STEPPING UP THEIR GAME.
I HOPE I'M NOT TOO LATE!

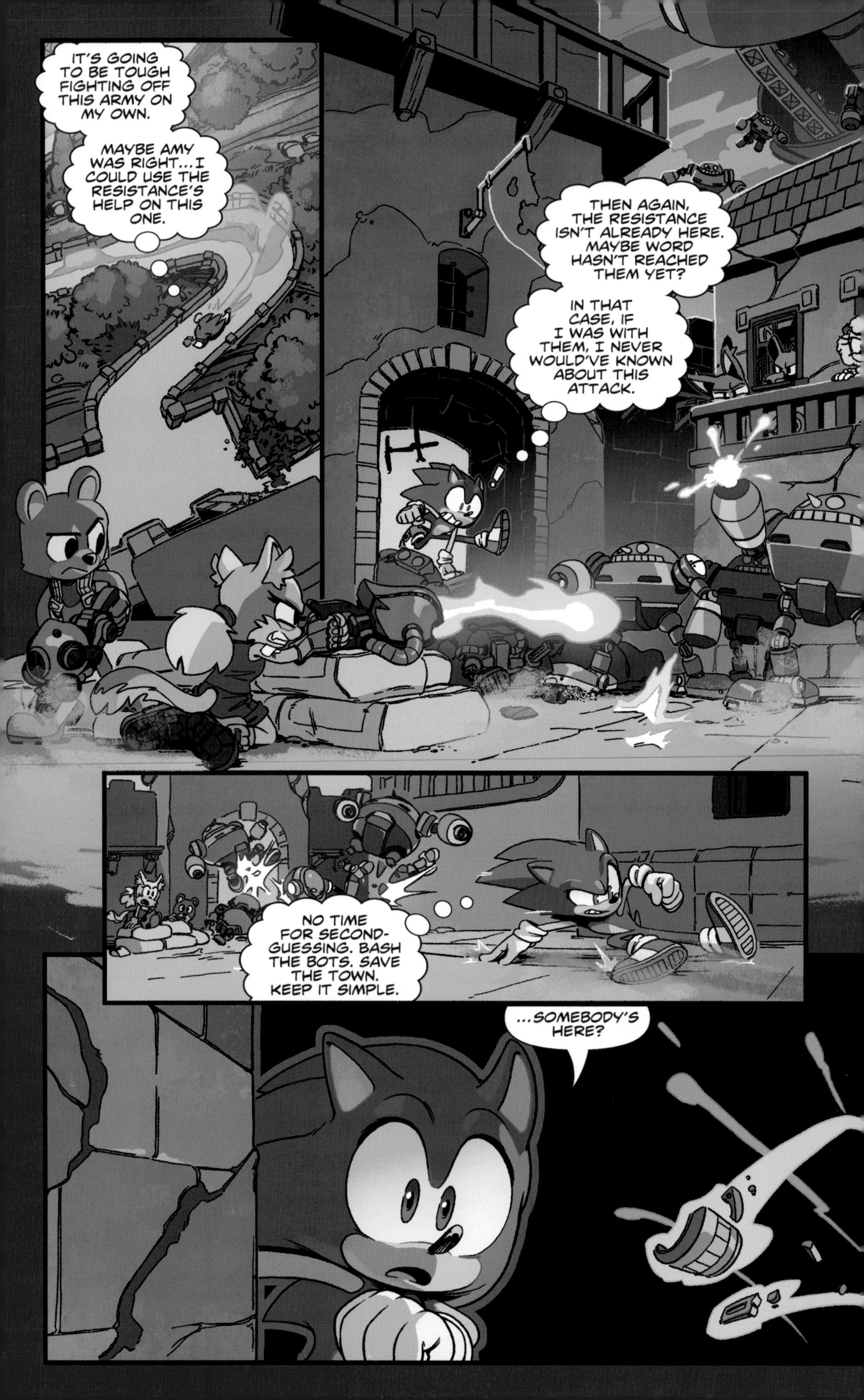
IT'S GOING TO BE TOUGH FIGHTING OFF THIS ARMY ON MY OWN.
MAYBE AMY WAS RIGHT... I COULD USE THE RESISTANCE'S HELP ON THIS ONE.
THEN AGAIN, THE RESISTANCE ISN'T ALREADY HERE. MAYBE WORD HASN'T REACHED THEM YET?
IN THAT CASE, IF I WAS WITH THEM, I NEVER WOULD'VE KNOWN ABOUT THIS ATTACK.
NO TIME FOR SECOND-GUESSING. BASH THE BOTS. SAVE THE TOWN. KEEP IT SIMPLE.
...SOMEBODY'S HERE?

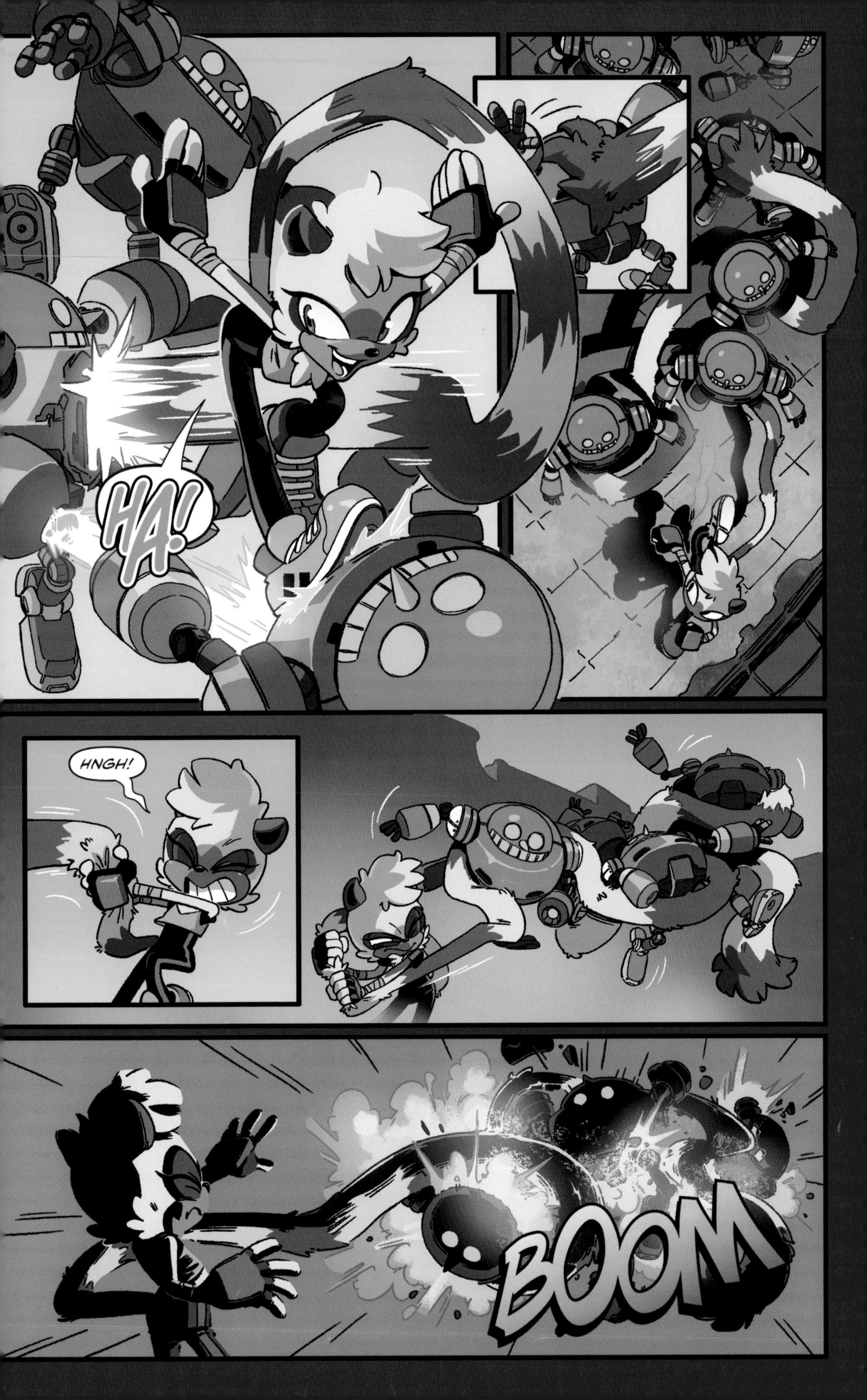
HA!
HNGH!
BOOM

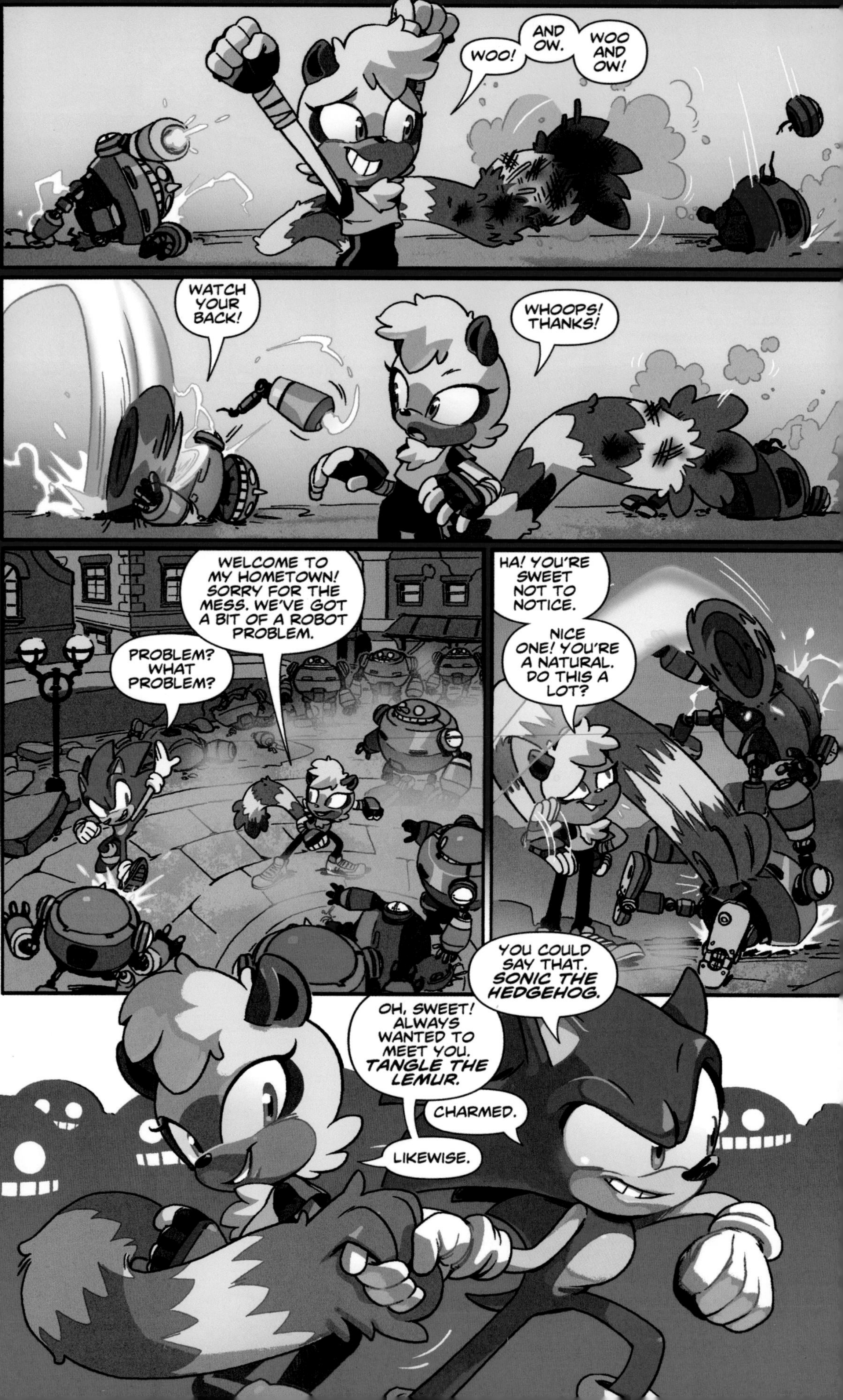
WOO!
AND OW.
WOO AND OW!
WATCH YOUR BACK!
WHOOPS! THANKS!
WELCOME TO MY HOMETOWN! SORRY FOR THE MESS. WE'VE GOT A BIT OF A ROBOT PROBLEM.
PROBLEM? WHAT PROBLEM?
HA! YOU'RE SWEET NOT TO NOTICE.
NICE ONE! YOU'RE A NATURAL. DO THIS A LOT?
YOU COULD SAY THAT. SONIC THE HEDGEHOG.
OH, SWEET! ALWAYS WANTED TO MEET YOU. TANGLE THE LEMUR.
CHARMED.
LIKEWISE.

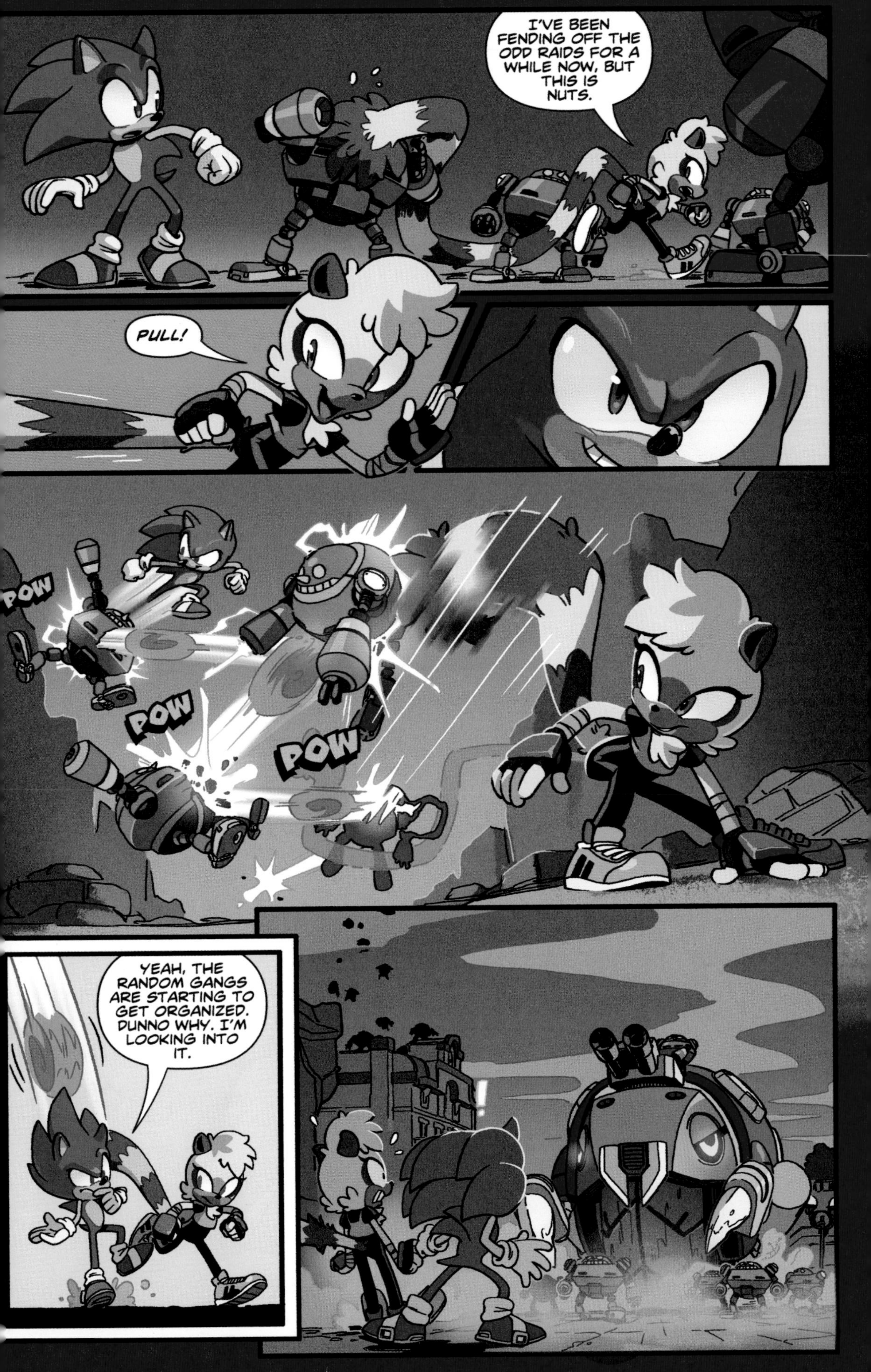
I'VE BEEN FENDING OFF THE ODD RAIDS FOR A WHILE NOW, BUT THIS IS NUTS.
PULL!
POW
POW
POW
YEAH, THE RANDOM GANGS ARE STARTING TO GET ORGANIZED. DUNNO WHY. I'M LOOKING INTO IT.
!

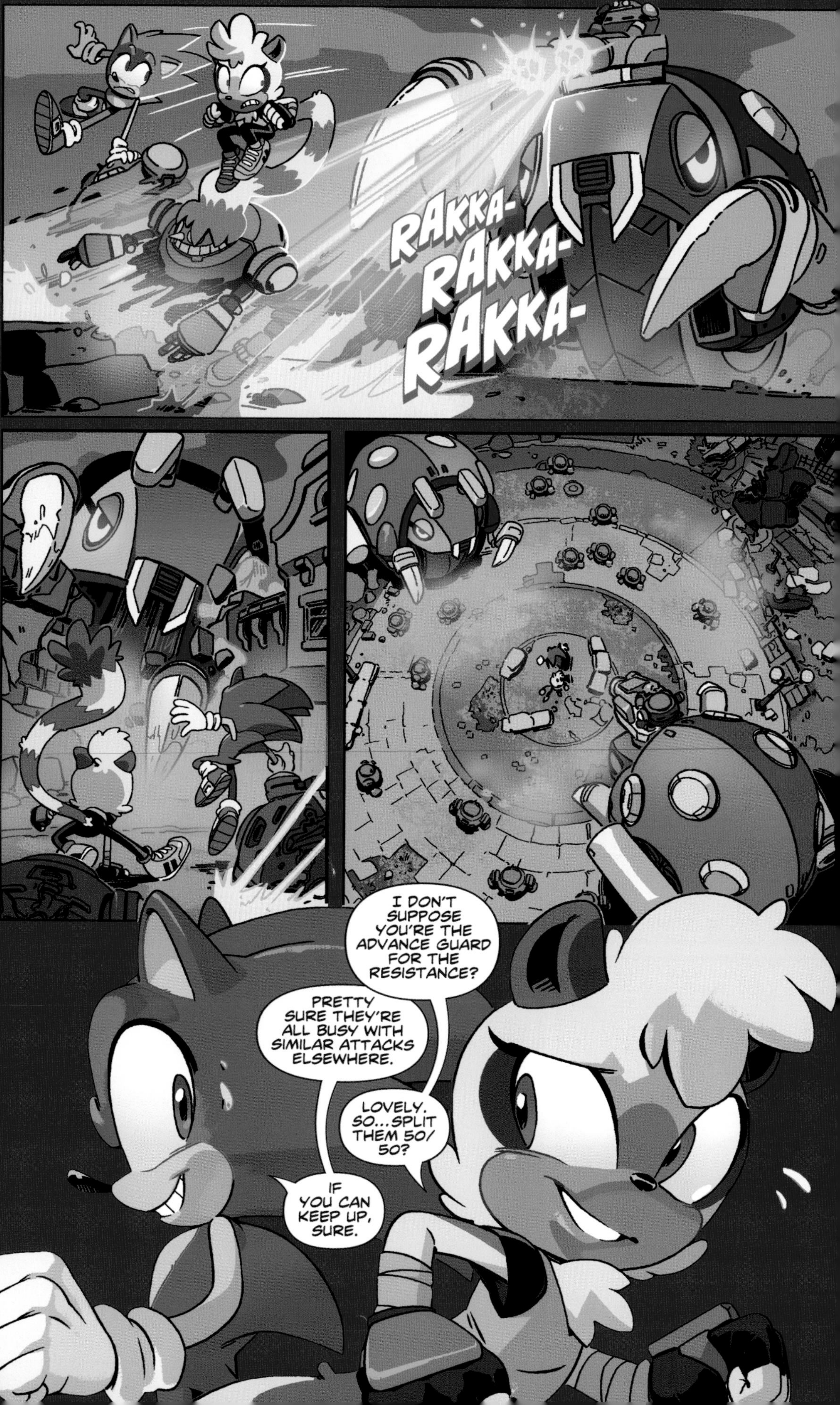
RAKKA-
RAKKA-
RAKKA-
I DON'T SUPPOSE YOU'RE THE ADVANCE GUARD FOR THE RESISTANCE?
PRETTY SURE THEY'RE ALL BUSY WITH SIMILAR ATTACKS ELSEWHERE.
LOVELY. SO...SPLIT THEM 50/50?
IF YOU CAN KEEP UP, SURE.

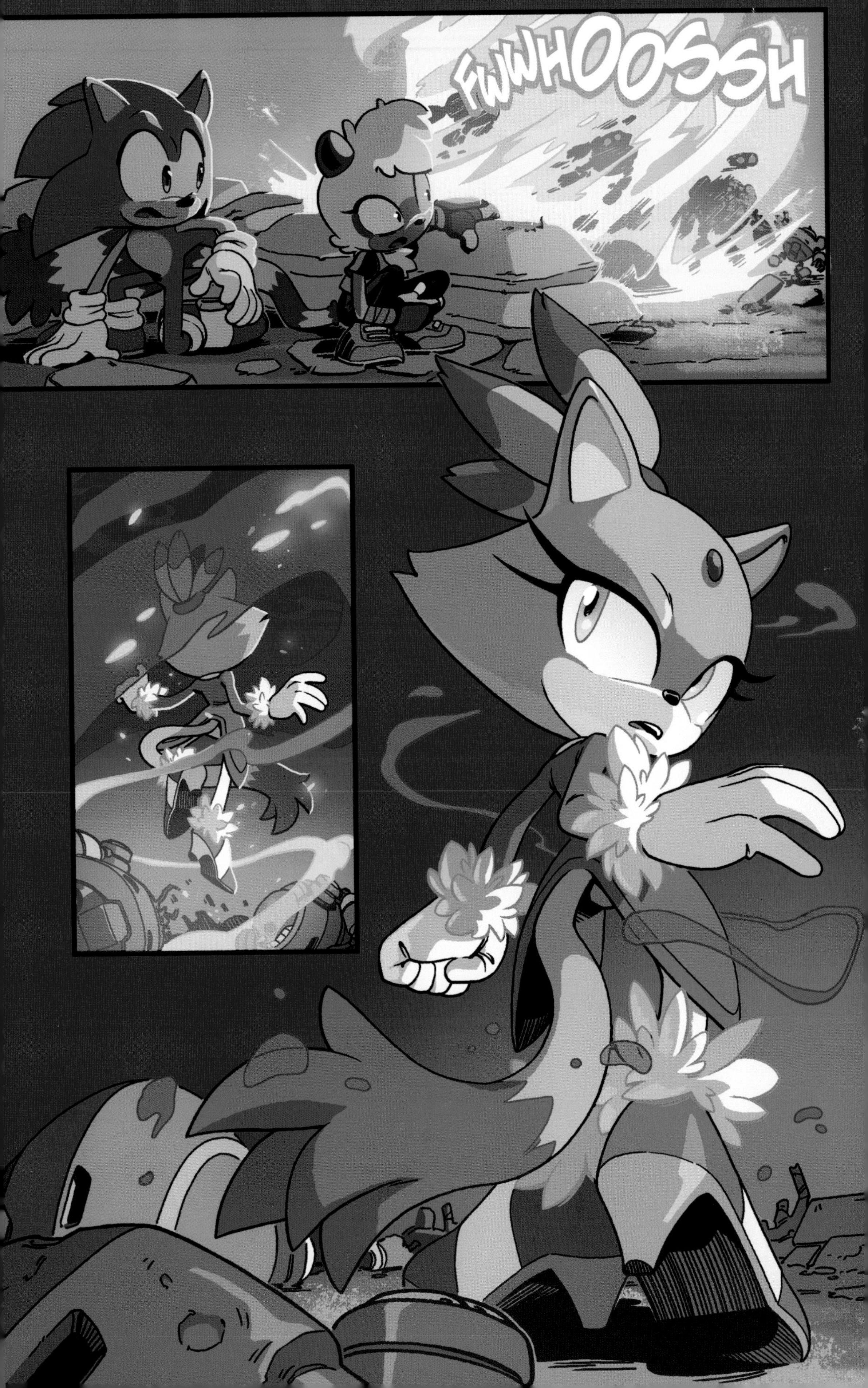
FWWHOOSSH

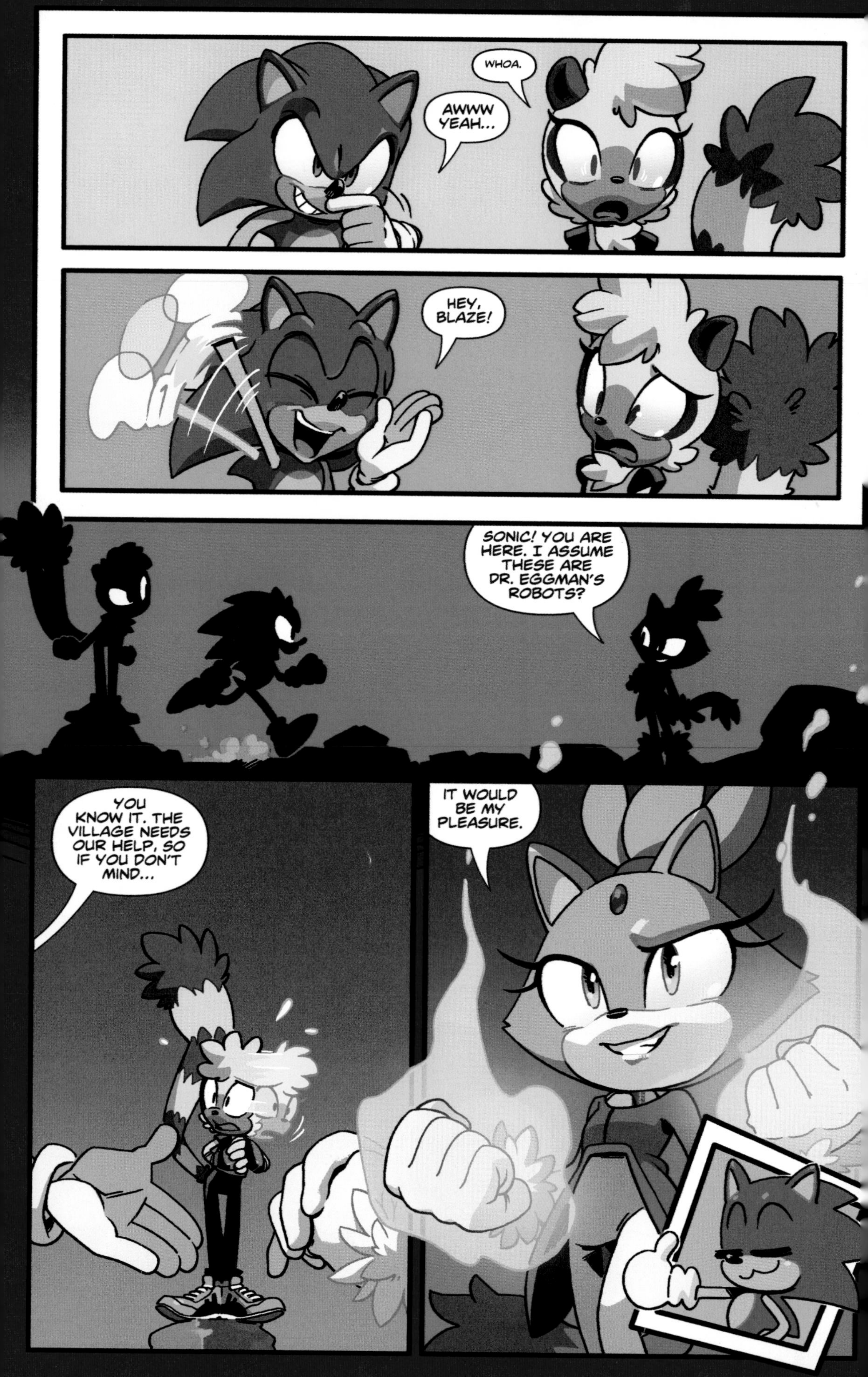
WHOA.
AWWW YEAH...
HEY, BLAZE!
SONIC! YOU ARE HERE. I ASSUME THESE ARE DR. EGGMAN'S ROBOTS?
YOU KNOW IT. THE VILLAGE NEEDS OUR HELP, SO IF YOU DON'T MIND...
IT WOULD BE MY PLEASURE.

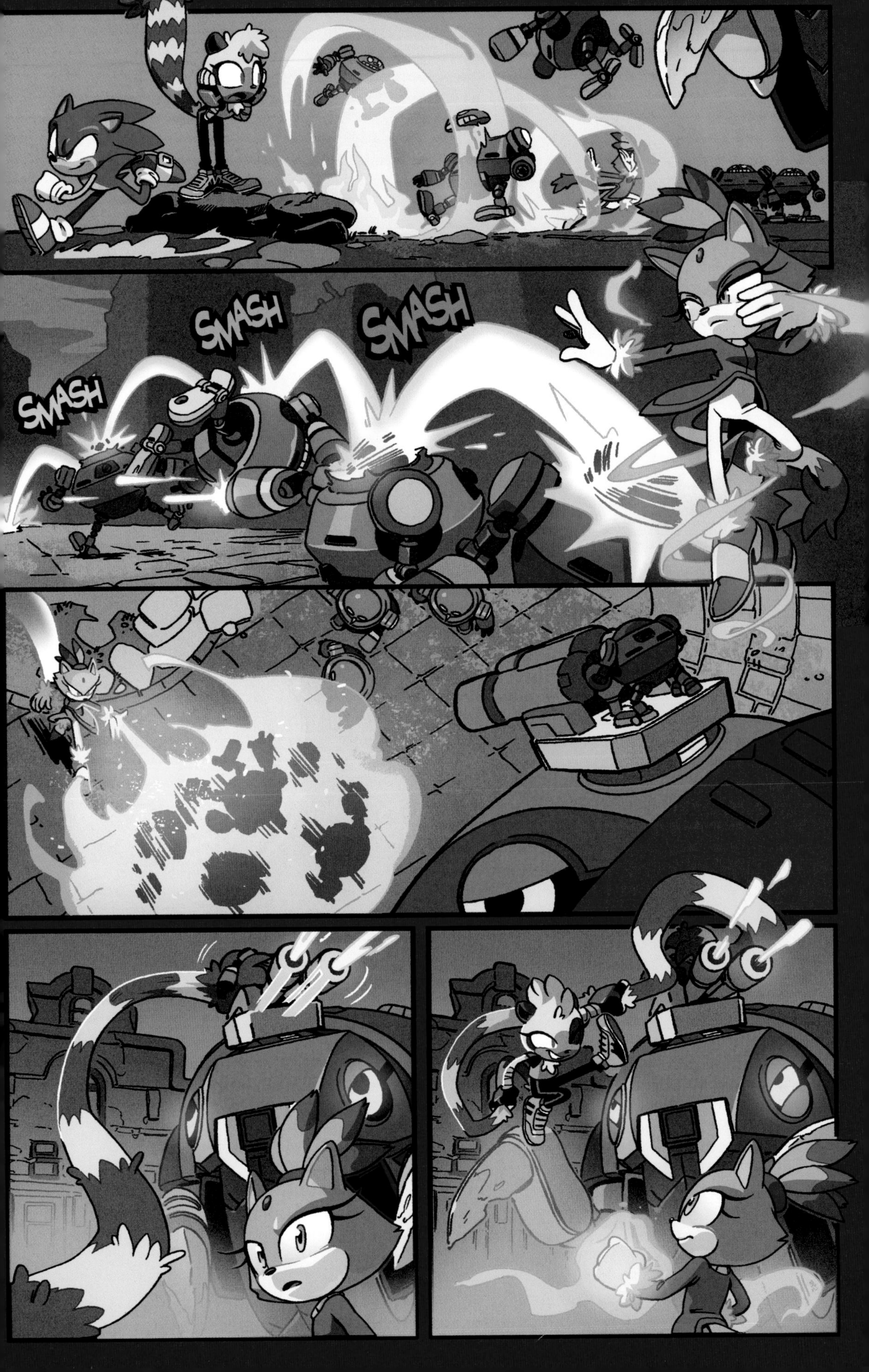
SMASH
SMASH
SMASH

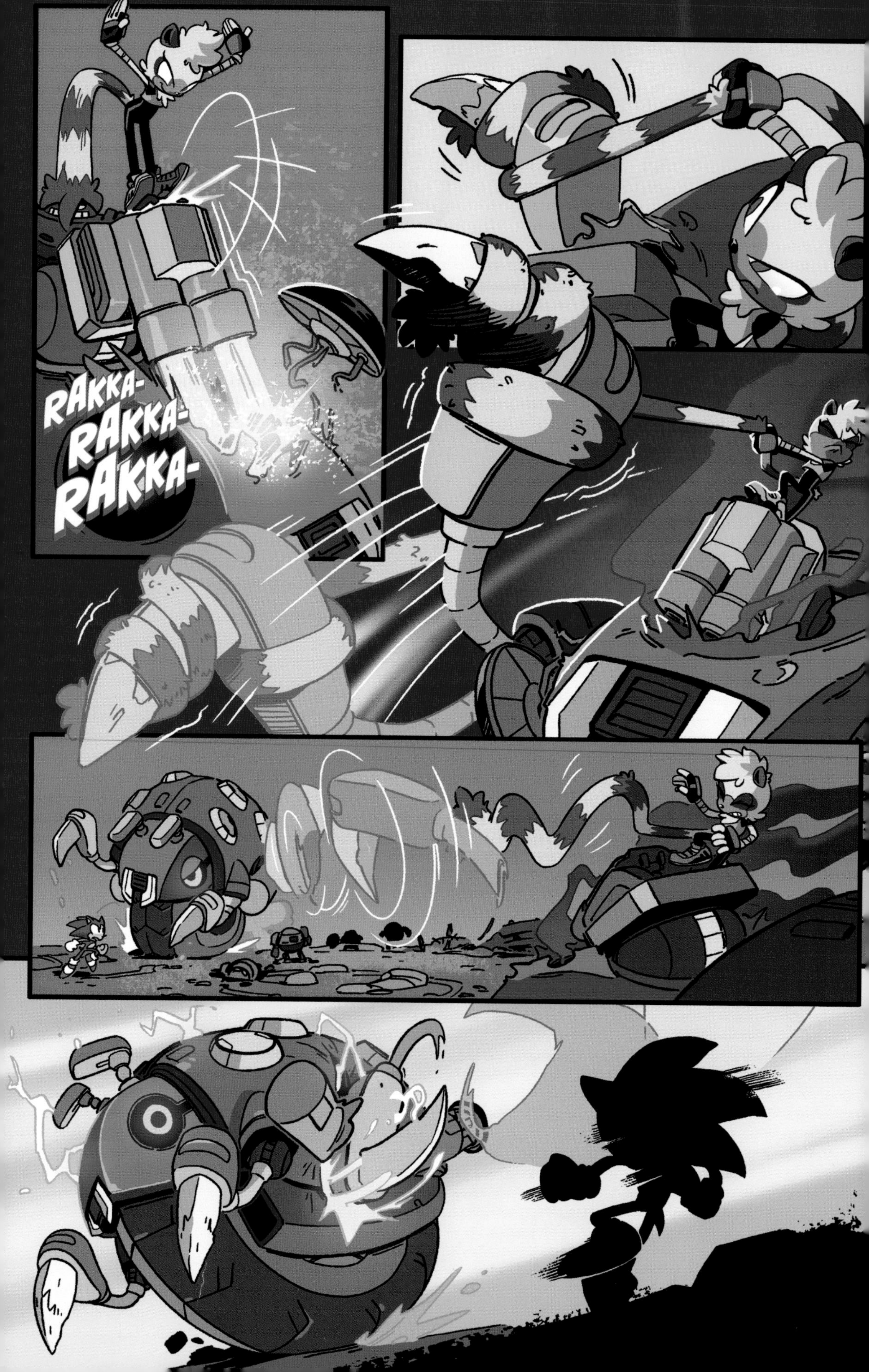
RAKKA-
RAKKA-
RAKKA-

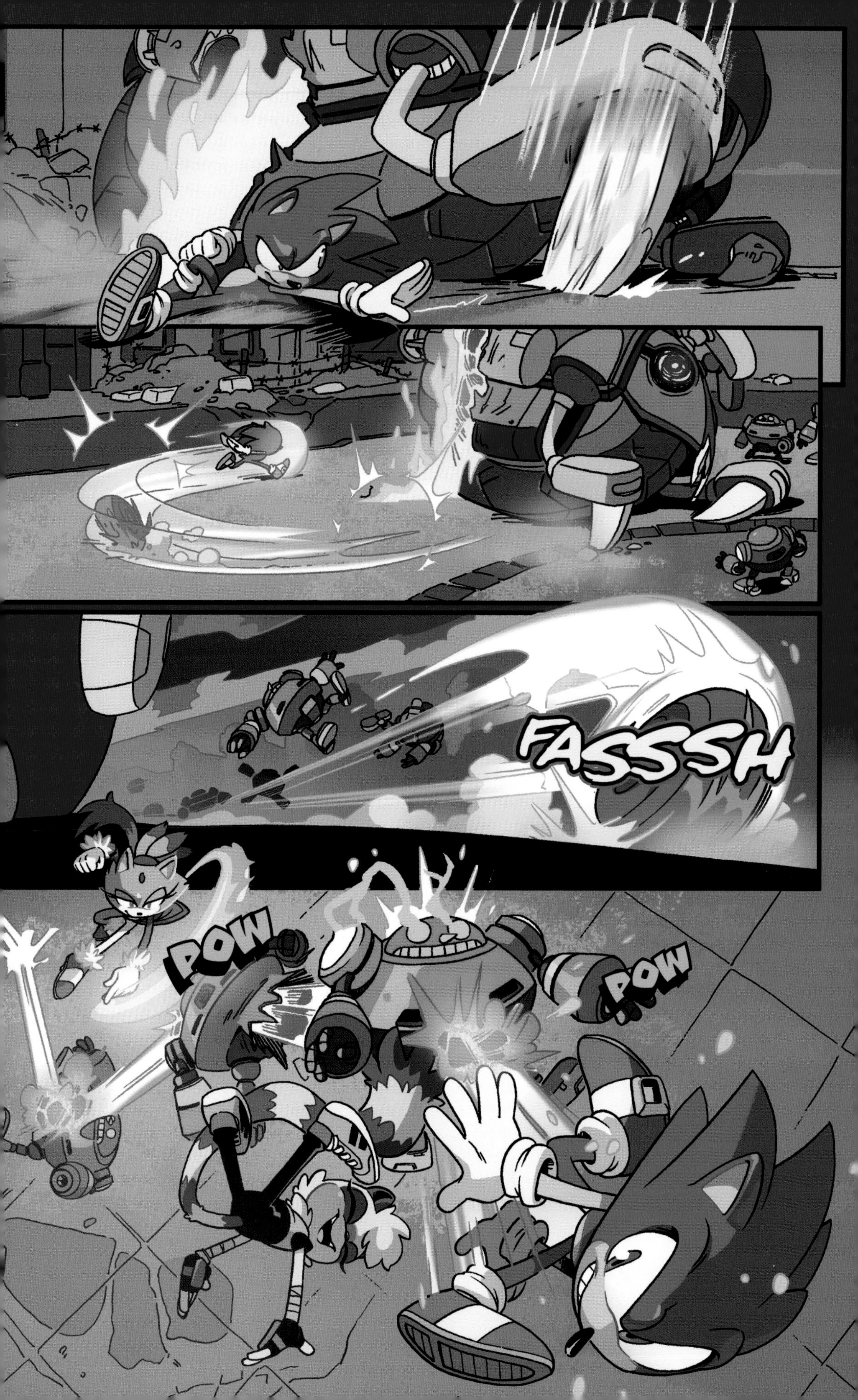
FASSSH
POW
POW

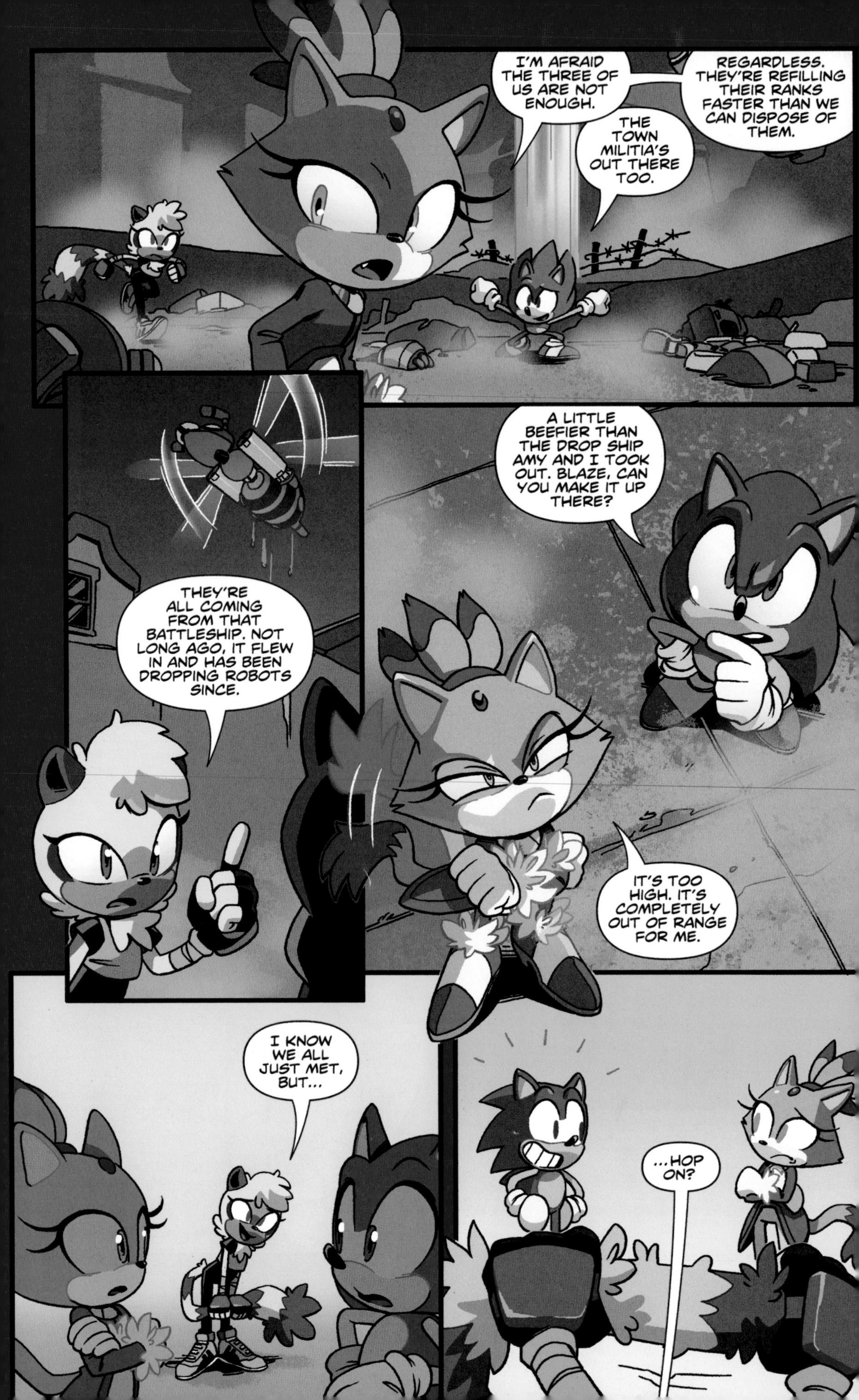
I'M AFRAID THE THREE OF US ARE NOT ENOUGH.
THE TOWN MILITIA'S OUT THERE TOO.
REGARDLESS. THEY'RE REFILLING THEIR RANKS FASTER THAN WE CAN DISPOSE OF THEM.
THEY'RE ALL COMING FROM THAT BATTLESHIP. NOT LONG AGO, IT FLEW IN AND HAS BEEN DROPPING ROBOTS SINCE.
A LITTLE BEEFIER THAN THE DROP SHIP AMY AND I TOOK OUT. BLAZE, CAN YOU MAKE IT UP THERE?
IT'S TOO HIGH. IT'S COMPLETELY OUT OF RANGE FOR ME.
I KNOW WE ALL JUST MET, BUT...
...HOP ON?

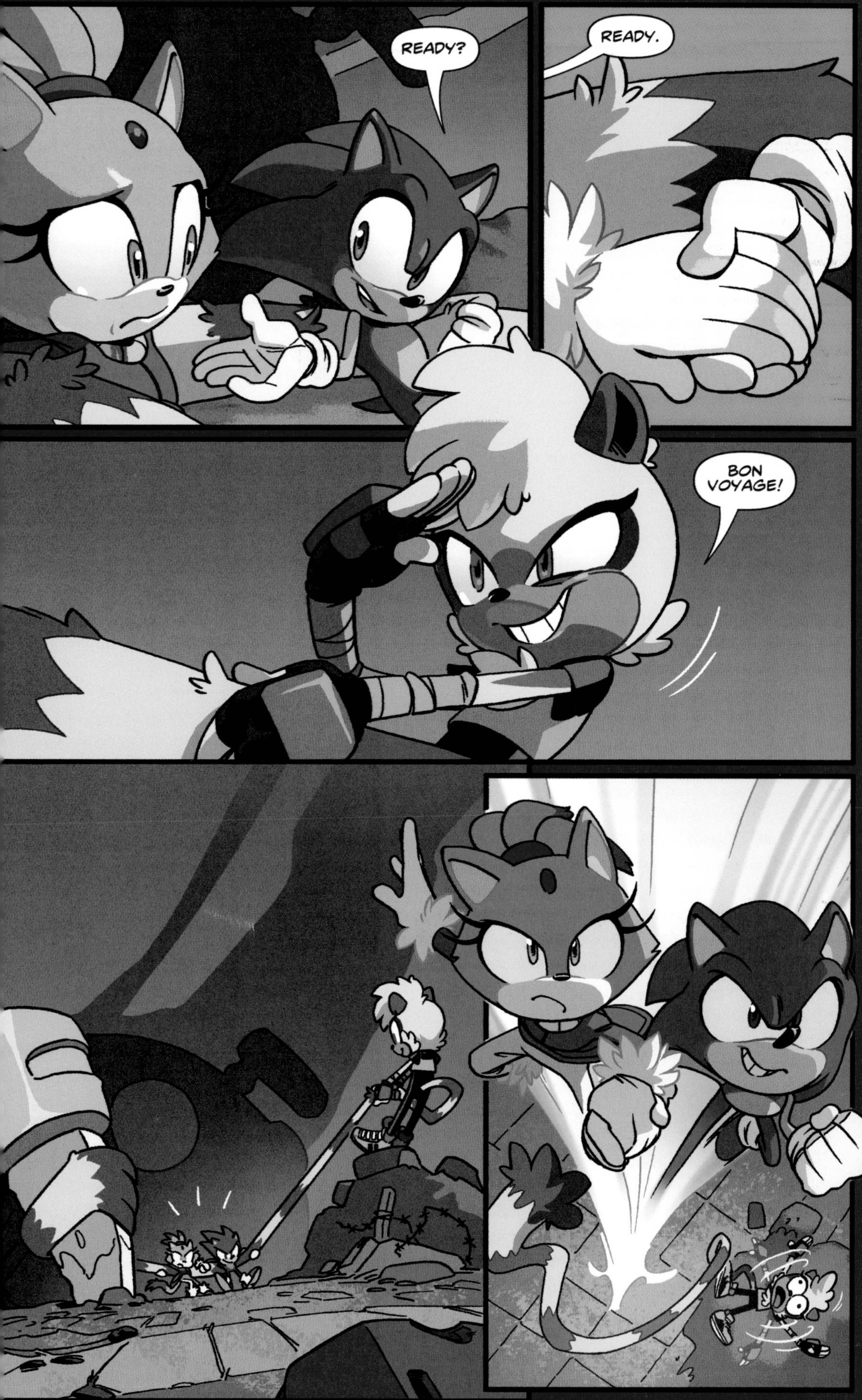
READY?
READY.
BON VOYAGE!

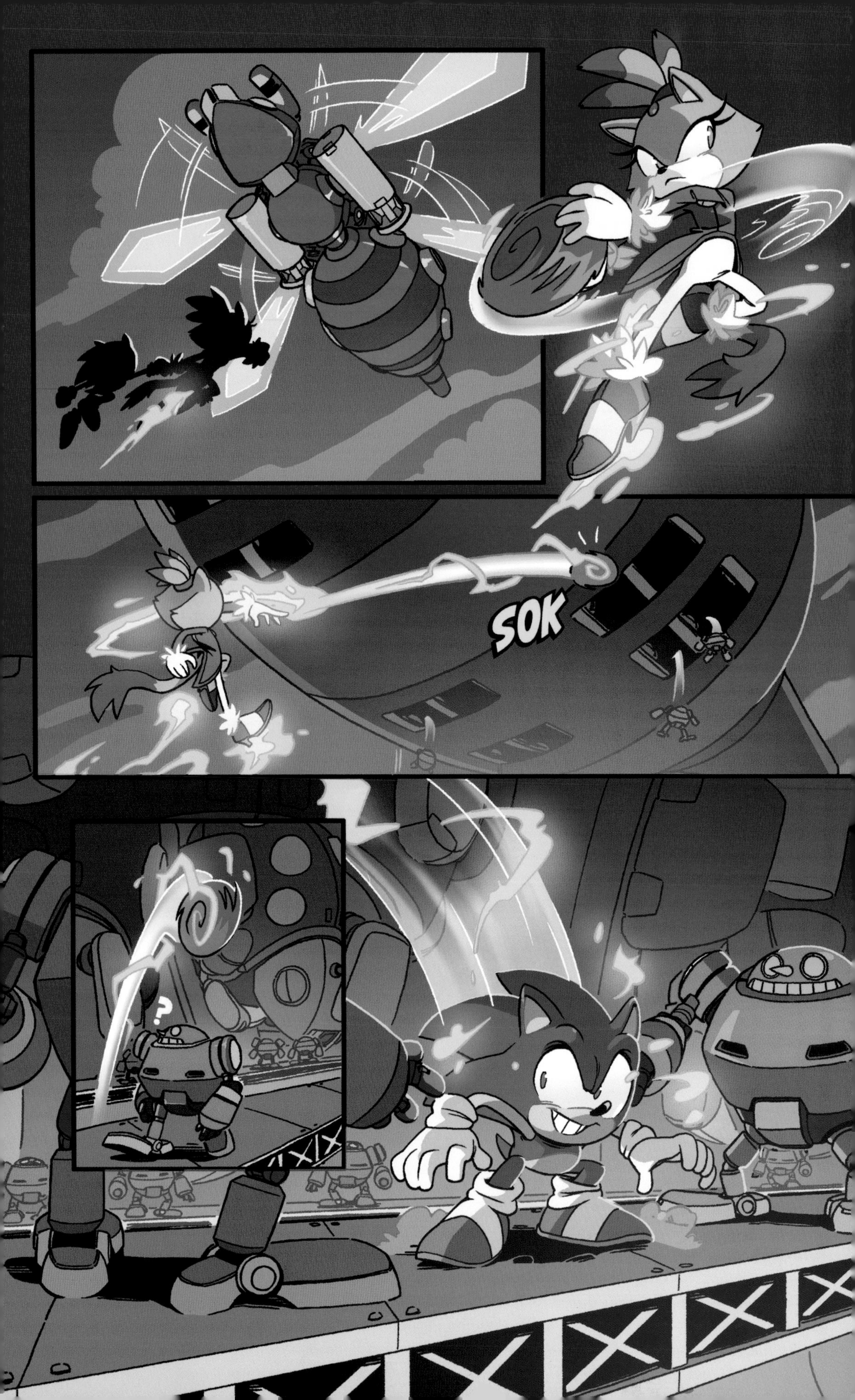
SOK
?

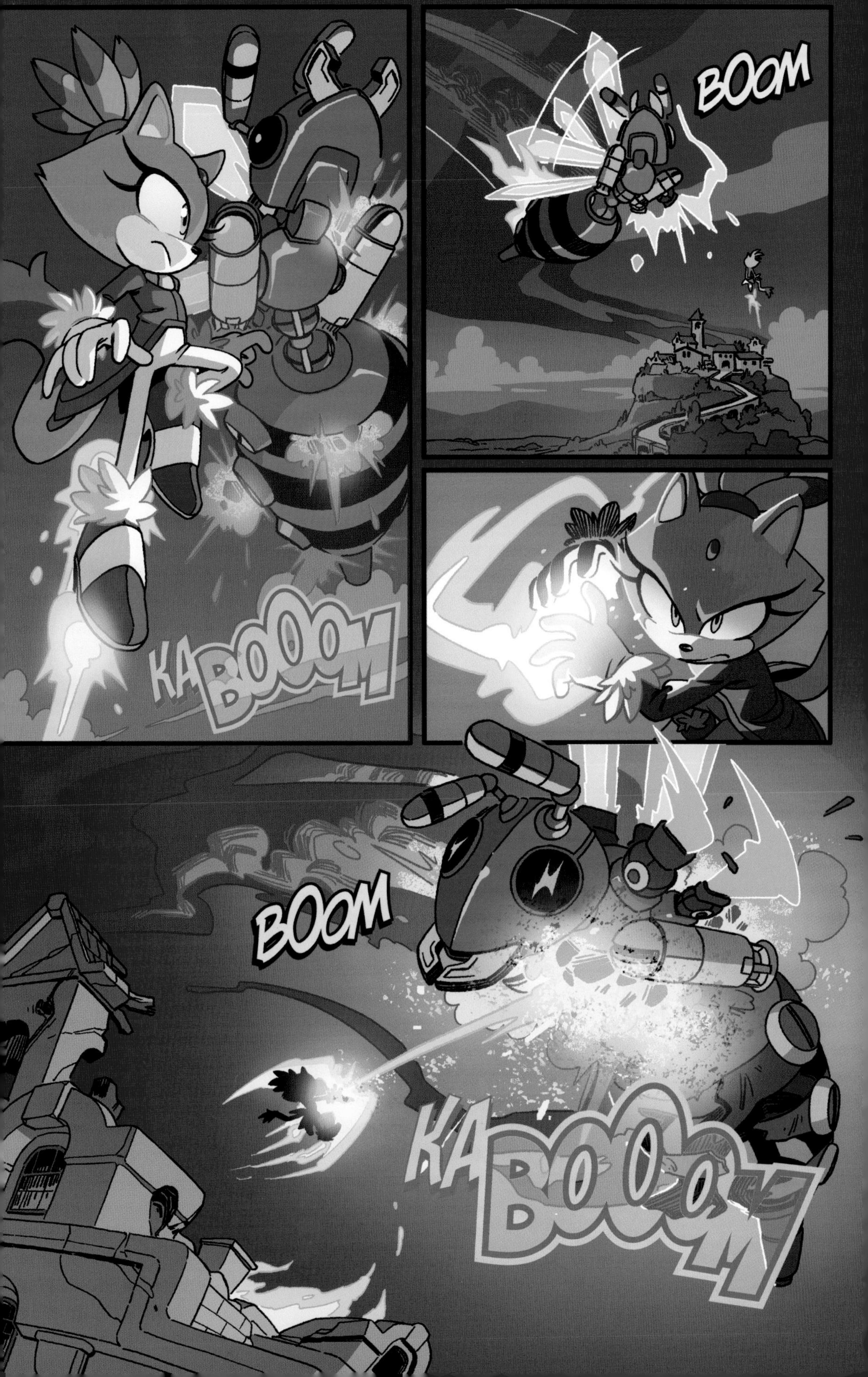
KABOOOM
BOOM
BOOM
KABOOOOM

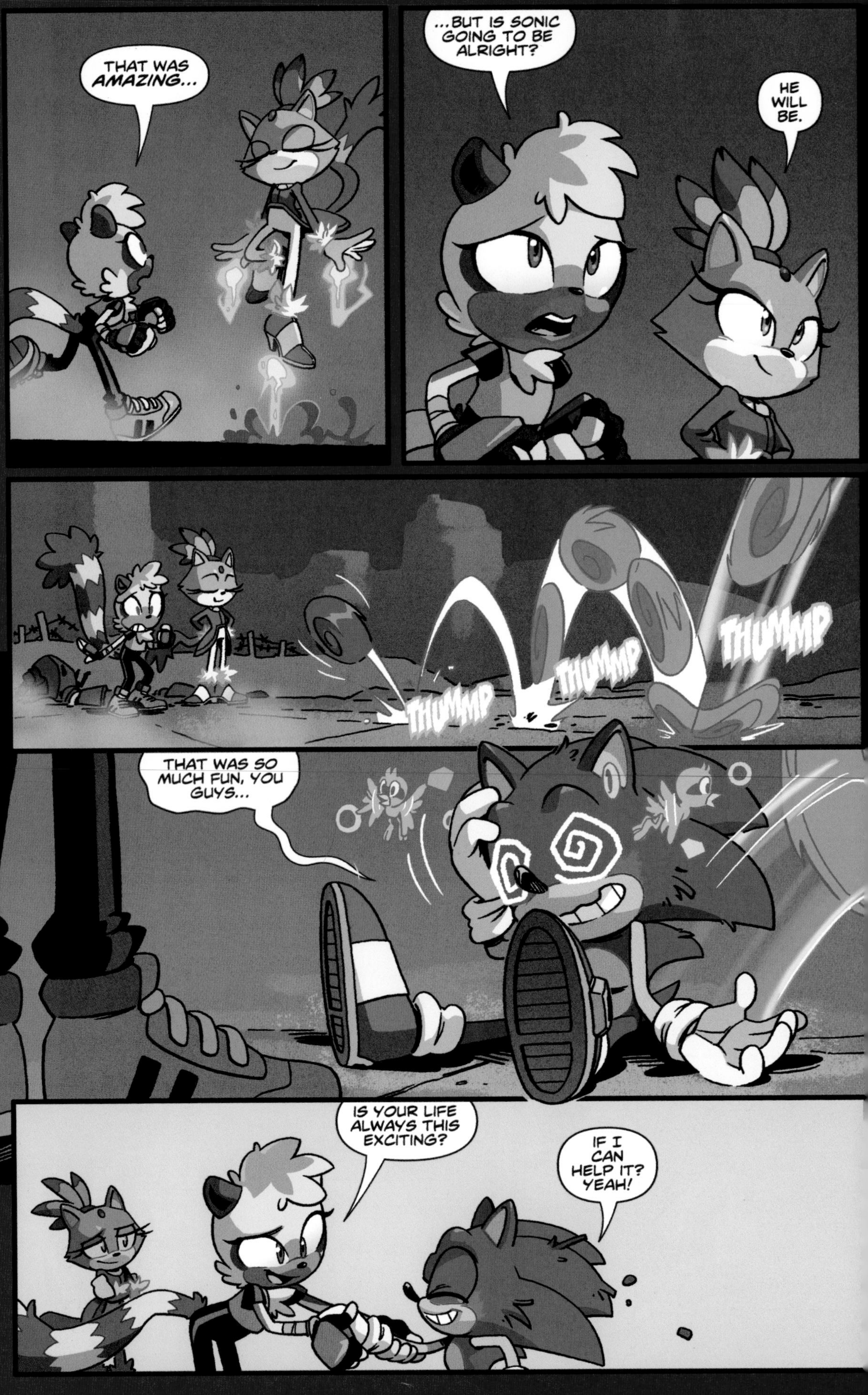
THAT WAS AMAZING...
...BUT IS SONIC GOING TO BE ALRIGHT?
HE WILL BE.
THUMMP
THUMMP
THUMMP
THAT WAS SO MUCH FUN, YOU GUYS...
IS YOUR LIFE ALWAYS THIS EXCITING?
IF I CAN HELP IT? YEAH!

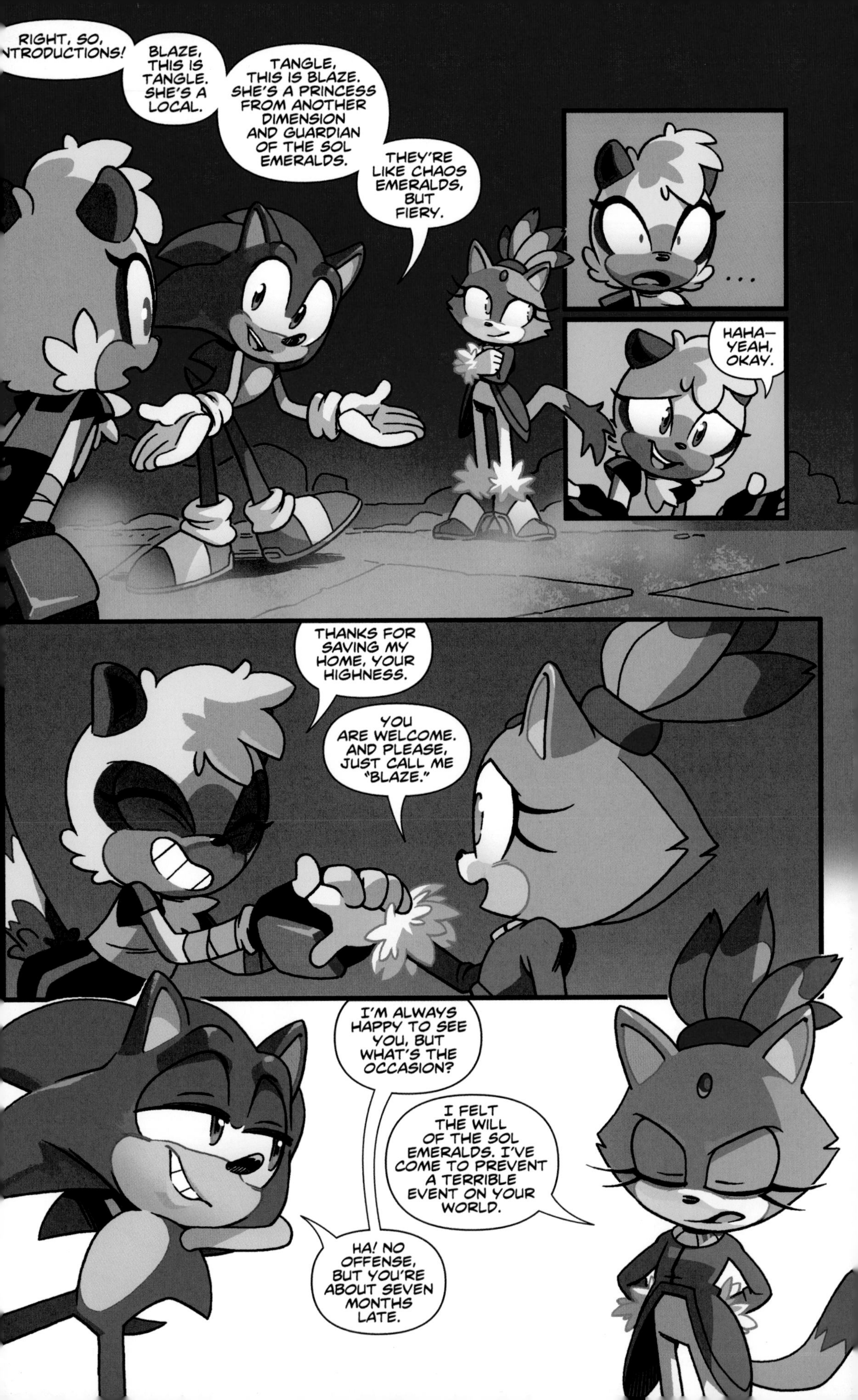
RIGHT, SO, INTRODUCTIONS!
BLAZE, THIS IS TANGLE. SHE'S A LOCAL.
TANGLE, THIS IS BLAZE. SHE'S A PRINCESS FROM ANOTHER DIMENSION AND GUARDIAN OF THE SOL EMERALDS.
THEY'RE LIKE CHAOS EMERALDS, BUT FIERY.
...
HAHA— YEAH, OKAY.
THANKS FOR SAVING MY HOME, YOUR HIGHNESS.
YOU ARE WELCOME. AND PLEASE, JUST CALL ME "BLAZE."
I'M ALWAYS HAPPY TO SEE YOU, BUT WHAT'S THE OCCASION?
I FELT THE WILL OF THE SOL EMERALDS. I'VE COME TO PREVENT A TERRIBLE EVENT ON YOUR WORLD.
HA! NO OFFENSE, BUT YOU'RE ABOUT SEVEN MONTHS LATE.

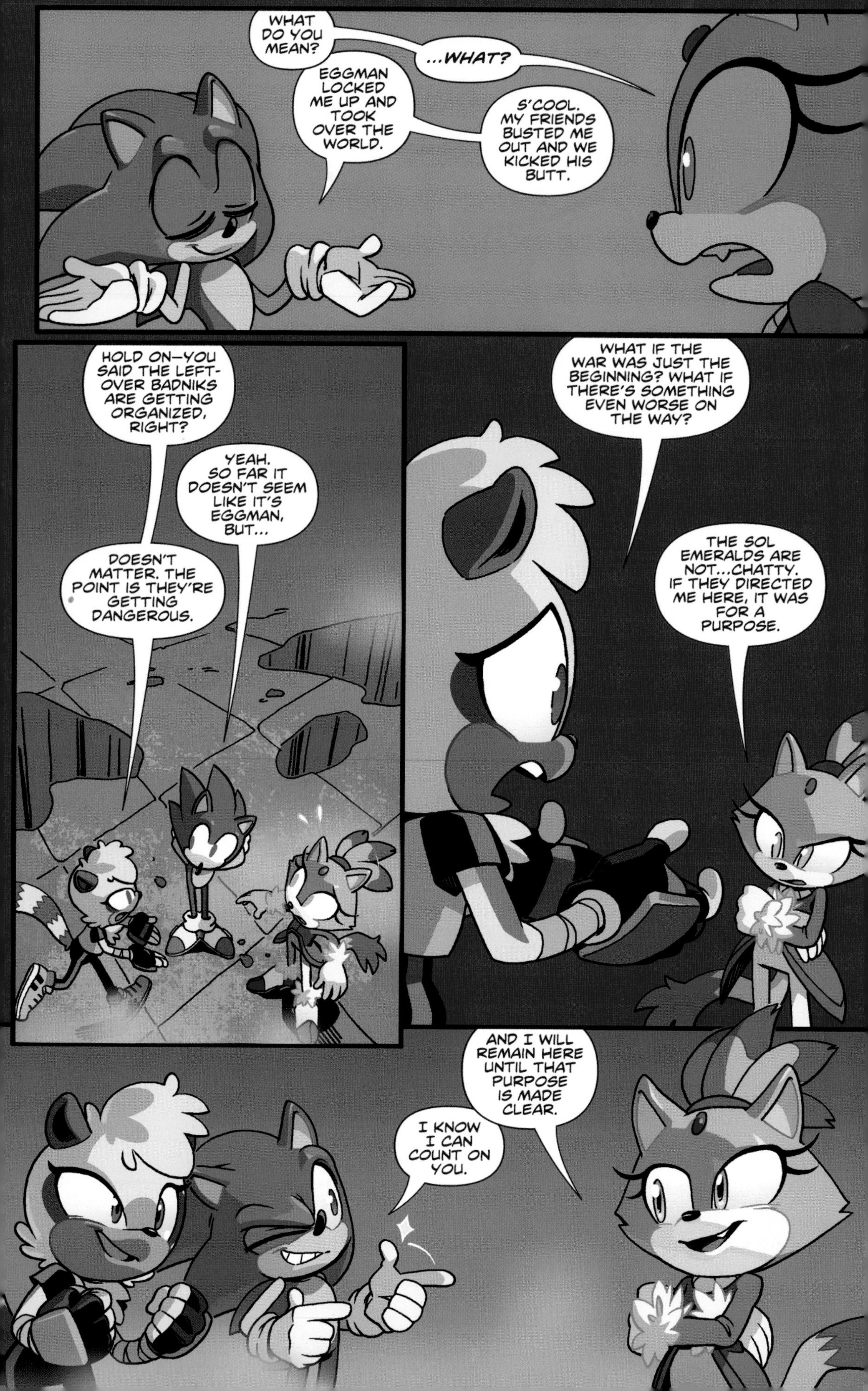
WHAT DO YOU MEAN?
EGGMAN LOCKED ME UP AND TOOK OVER THE WORLD.
...WHAT?
S'COOL. MY FRIENDS BUSTED ME OUT AND WE KICKED HIS BUTT.
HOLD ON—YOU SAID THE LEFT-OVER BADNIKS ARE GETTING ORGANIZED, RIGHT?
YEAH. SO FAR IT DOESN'T SEEM LIKE IT'S EGGMAN, BUT...
DOESN'T MATTER. THE POINT IS THEY'RE GETTING DANGEROUS.
WHAT IF THE WAR WAS JUST THE BEGINNING? WHAT IF THERE'S SOMETHING EVEN WORSE ON THE WAY?
THE SOL EMERALDS ARE NOT...CHATTY. IF THEY DIRECTED ME HERE, IT WAS FOR A PURPOSE.
AND I WILL REMAIN HERE UNTIL THAT PURPOSE IS MADE CLEAR.
I KNOW I CAN COUNT ON YOU.

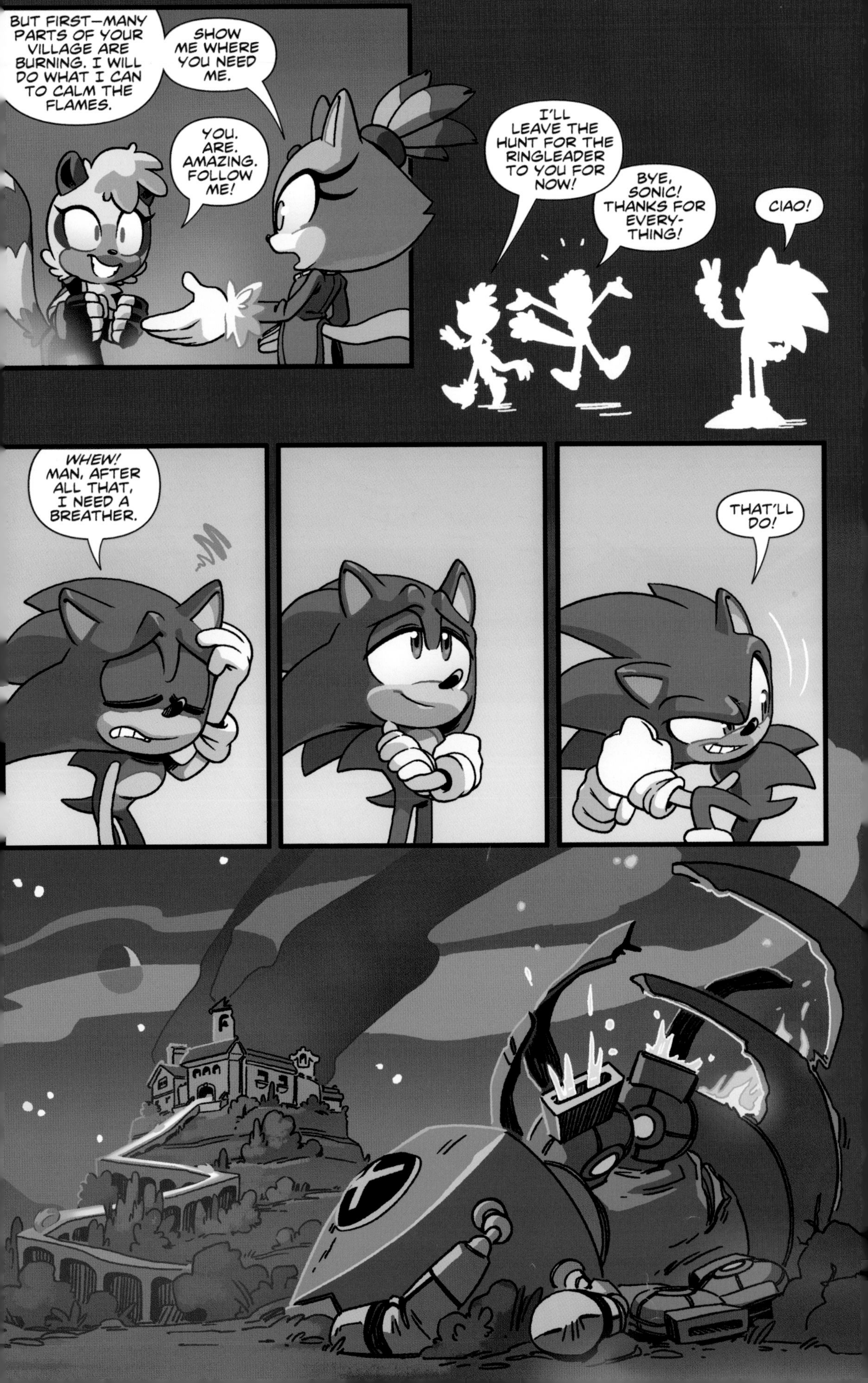

BUT FIRST—MANY PARTS OF YOUR VILLAGE ARE BURNING. I WILL DO WHAT I CAN TO CALM THE FLAMES.
SHOW ME WHERE YOU NEED ME.
YOU. ARE. AMAZING. FOLLOW ME!
I'LL LEAVE THE HUNT FOR THE RINGLEADER TO YOU FOR NOW!
BYE, SONIC! THANKS FOR EVERY-THING!
CIAO!
WHEW! MAN, AFTER ALL THAT, I NEED A BREATHER.
THAT'LL DO!

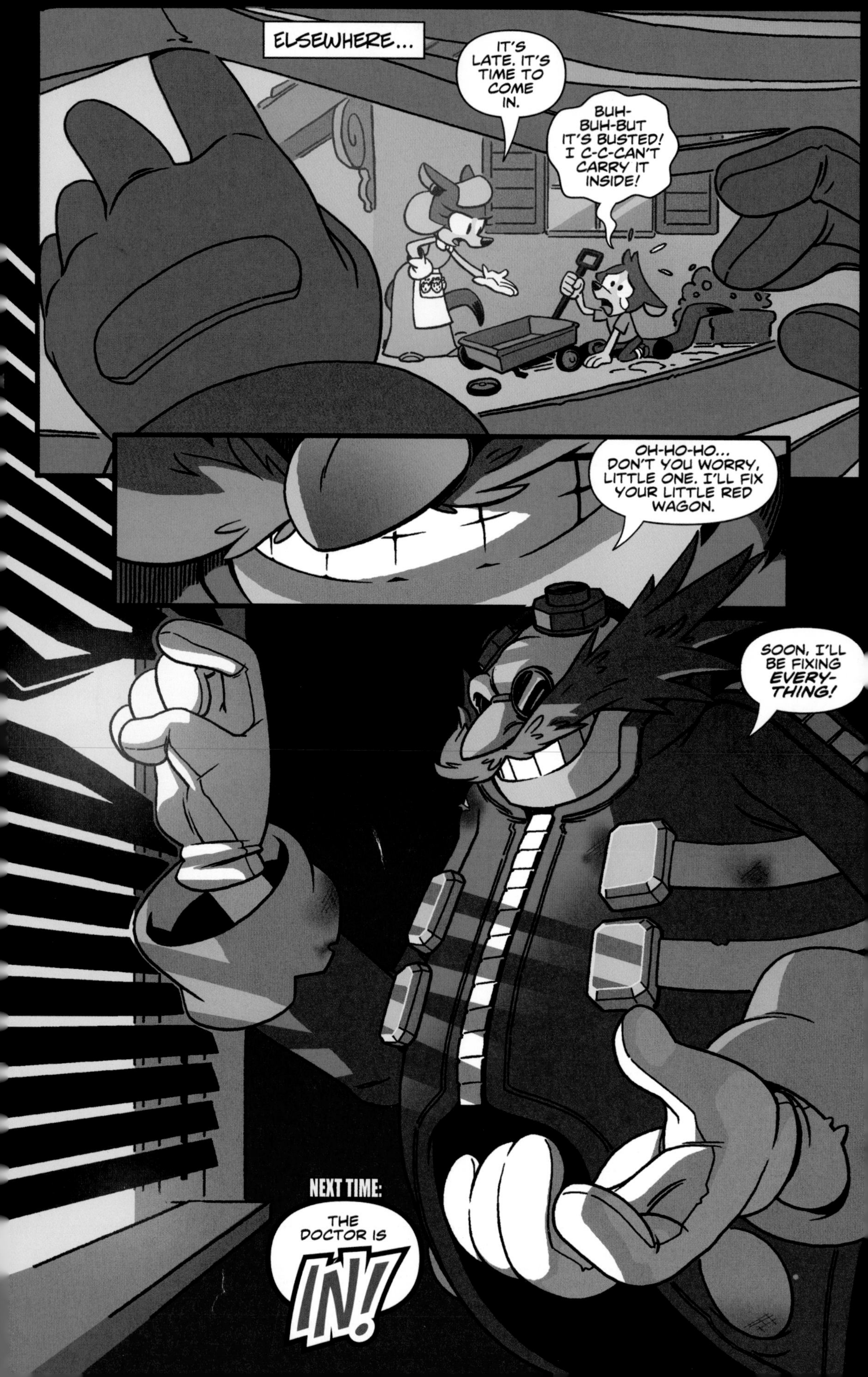
ELSEWHERE...
IT'S LATE. IT'S TIME TO COME IN.
BUH-BUH-BUT IT'S BUSTED! I C-C-CAN'T CARRY IT INSIDE!
OH-HO-HO... DON'T YOU WORRY, LITTLE ONE. I'LL FIX YOUR LITTLE RED WAGON.
SOON, I'LL BE FIXING EVERY-THING!
NEXT TIME:
THE DOCTOR IS IN!

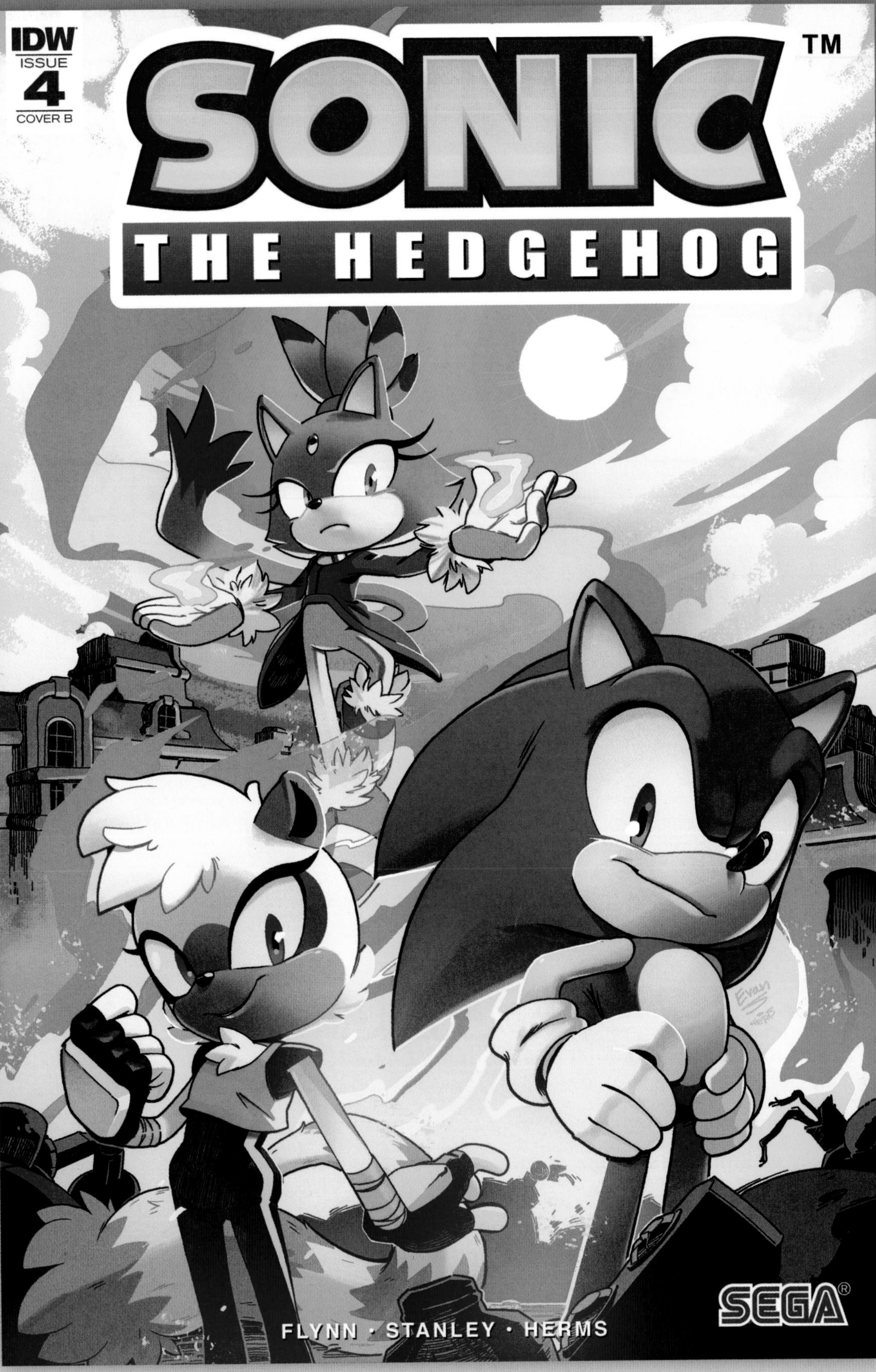
IDW
ISSUE
4
COVER B
SONIC
THE HEDGEHOG
TM
SEGA
FLYNN · STANLEY · HERMS

COVER B

ART BY EVAN STANLEY COLORS BY MATT HERMS

COLLECT THEM ALL!

Set of 6 Hardcover Books ISBN: 978-1-5321-4432-5

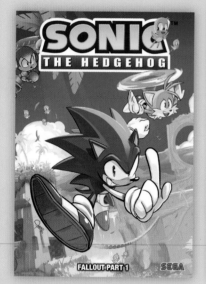

Hardcover Book ISBN
978-1-5321-4433-2

Hardcover Book ISBN
978-1-5321-4434-9

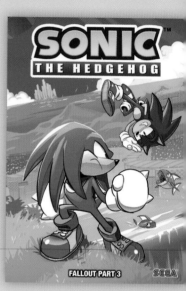

Hardcover Book ISBN
978-1-5321-4435-6

Hardcover Book ISBN
978-1-5321-4436-3

Hardcover Book ISBN
978-1-5321-4437-0

Hardcover Book ISBN
978-1-5321-4438-7